Because we all need a good daily dose of laughter!

D.A.

Hardcover ISBN: 978-1-953118-24-0
Paperback ISBN: 978-1-953118-25-7

Library of Congress Control Number: 2022916152

Published by Dedoni, LLC
www.dedonibooks.com

THE NAUGHTY SHEEP

Diana Aleksandrova

Anna Burak

I toss and turn; I cannot sleep.
I close my eyes and count some sheep:

THREE SHEEP...

With tutu and ballet shoes, too,
the fourth sheep makes her way right through.

A skip, a leap, a jump, and prance...

Soon comes a hop and then a dance.

Pirouette she does instead

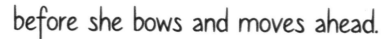

before she bows and moves ahead.

No time to wonder what was that . . .
The sheep is now an acrobat.
First, cartwheels and a somersault—
A split, and then a sudden halt.

Hey, sheep!
You really must
admit
I'm not yet
sleepy. Not one
bit!

The sheep pulls out a clarinet,
not knowing if I'll laugh or fret.

I start to hear a piercing squeak.
It's very shrill, just like a shriek.

Hey sheep,
you're such a loud musician.
Maybe, find another mission.

The sheep holds plates on one thin stick.
Is this a circus? What a trick!

The sheep sticks out its tongue that's blue.
She winks and gestures 'peek-a-boo.'
Why can't you act like normal sheep?
I really, REALLY need to sleep!

She's gone away;
she heard my calls.
But now she's back . . .
and juggling balls!

You naughty sheep!
I'm still awake!
Did candy make you wild?
Or cake?

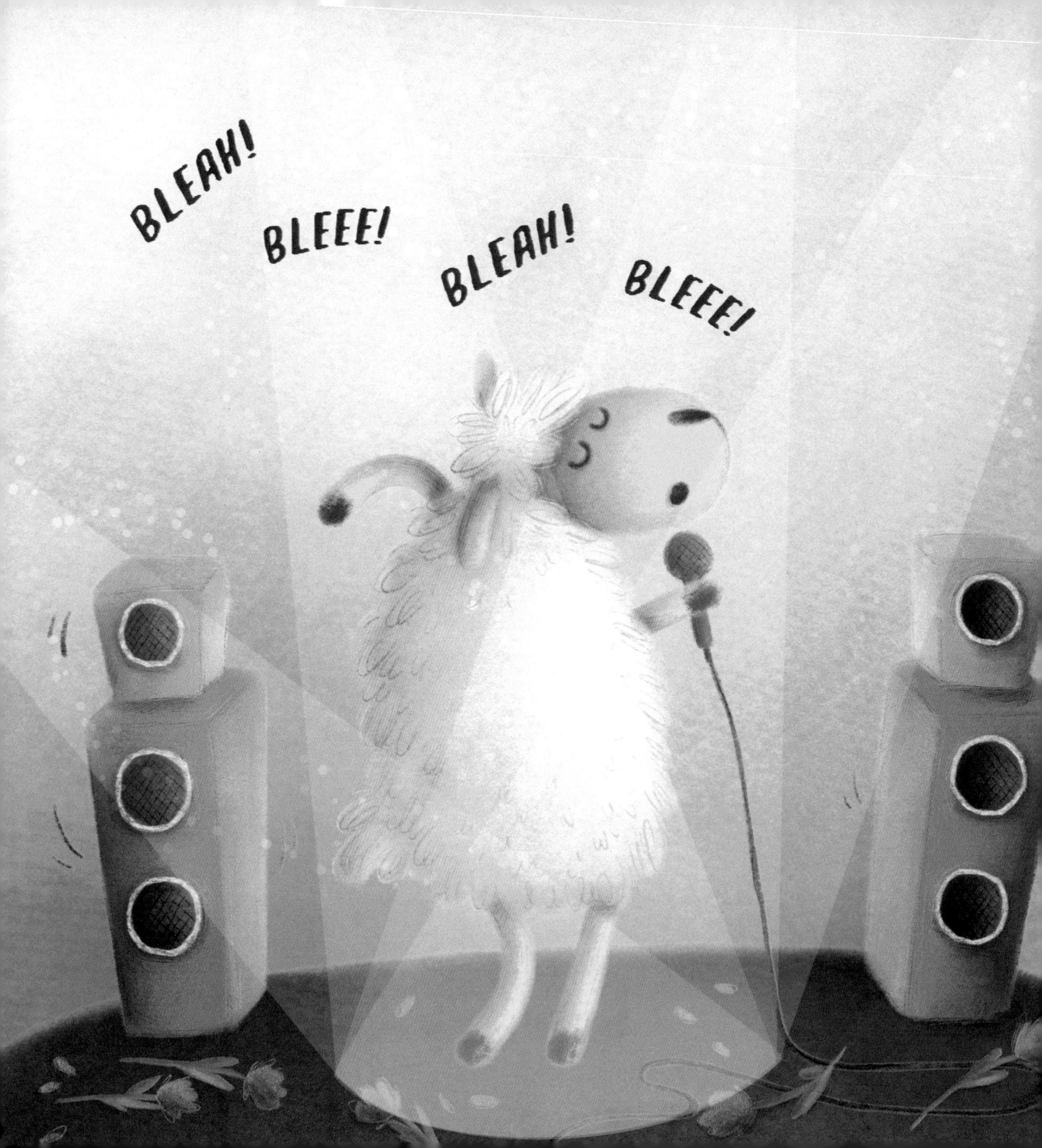
BLEAH!
BLEEE!
BLEAH!
BLEEE!

The sheep is singing karaoke—
noisy and extremely croaky!
Sheep, there's something else to try.
Hey, how about a lullaby?

I'm oh, so tired; that sheep can tell.
She calls the others with a bell:

ONE sheep.
TWO sheep.
THREE sheep . . .

My new friend yawns, and so do I.
Then, finally, she waves 'goodbye.'

But WAIT! Before you have to go,
there's something that I want to know:

How do sheep go to sleep?
Do they count OTHER sheep?

Diana Aleksandrova is award-winning author of children books.

Diana's mission is to help emerging and reluctant readers fall in love with books.

She believes that reading is the way to shape thinking and emotionally intelligent future generation.

The way to accomplish that is to give children books they would love; books that make them laugh and wonder.

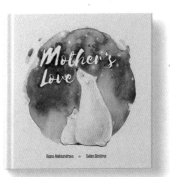

You can reach Diana at dedonibooks.com

Want more giggles?

After THE NAUGHTY SHEEP comes HOW DO SHEEP GO TO SLEEP?

When we can't sleep we count some sheep. But have you ever wonder how do sheep go to sleep? Do they count other sheep? Do sheep brush their teeth before bed? Do they wear PJs or nightgowns?

Those and other hilarious possibilities in
HOW DO SHEEP GO TO SLEEP?!

Made in the USA
Middletown, DE
13 April 2023